時差

多和田葉子

YOKO TAWADA

time DiFFeReNces

Translated by Jeffrey Angles

UEA PUBLISHING PROJECT
NORWICH

Time Differences
Yoko Tawada

Translated from the Japanese by
Jeffrey Angles

First published by
Strangers Press, Norwich, 2017
part of UEA Publishing Project

Distributed by
NBN International

Printed by
Swallowtail Print, Norwich

All rights reserved
© Yoko Tawada, 2006
Translation © Jeffrey Angles, 2017

Series editors
Elmer Luke
David Karashima

Editorial team
Kate Griffin
Nathan Hamilton
Philip Langeskov

Cover design and typesetting
Nigel Aono-Billson
Glen Robinson

Photography and Design © Glen Robinson, 2017

The rights of Yoko Tawada to be identified as the author and Jeffrey Angles identified as the translator of this work have been asserted in accordance with the Copyright, Designs and Patents Act, 1988. This booklet is sold subject to the condition that it shall not, by way of trade or otherwise, be lent, resold, hired out, stored in a retrieval system, or otherwise circulated without the publisher's prior consent in any form of binding or cover other than that in which it is published and without a similar condition including this condition being imposed on the subsequent purchaser.

ISBN-13: 978-1911343011

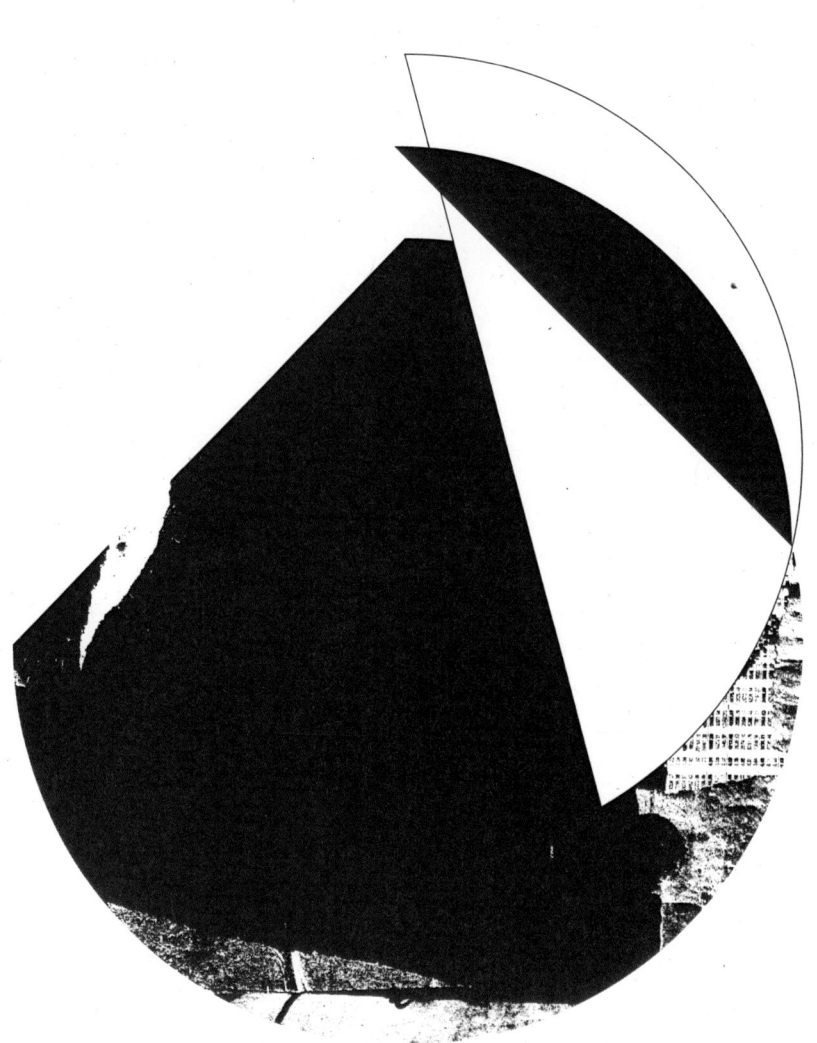

foreword

The simultaneity of the ménage-à-trois point of view is my favourite feature of this story by Yoko Tawada, who makes her home in Berlin where she writes in German as well as Japanese. This ingenuity of form adds an impressive compression to the story's 10,000 words in which we inhabit three sensibilities, three teeming modern cities, and a globalized world in which telephones are what connect and extend the few moments of physical intimacy. Here is disassociation, dislocation on several levels, postmodern life as we have come to know it.

The middle-class characters of three countries – none of them living in their own – are privileged with mobility even as they are a little flat. None seem particularly swept away by a passion for what they are doing, and their relationships are remote. So far as the ending is concerned, no spoiler alert is necessary, as given the theme of dislocation and the isolation inherent in the resulting disembodied relationships, conventional closure would be emotionally fraudulent.

If I didn't know *Time Differences* was a translation from the Japanese, it would never have occurred to me that the story wasn't originally written in English – so familiar is the sense of it in a culture half the world away. The writing itself is totally convincing and wonderfully agile. And how naturally it reads.

Stuart Dybek

MAMORU

ManFreD

MICHAEL

11

"Nine O'clock." The alarm on the radio switched on, and the low voice of a woman filled the room. Mamoru opened his eyes. "This is the news." He heard place names in Israel, numbers of casualties – then the announcer skipped to domestic German news as if there were no other countries in the world: Growing problems with the insurance system, rising unemployment, goals scored on the soccer field. Then the weather report: cloudy today with occasional rain, possibility of showers. In the traffic updates, Mamoru heard the names of towns he hadn't heard of before. Until a few years ago, he'd wonder how there could possibly be congestion between such small towns – after all, most people never visited those places in their entire lives.

The dark bread with sunflower seeds had grown hard, five days' worth of dry. The red currant jelly was covered with white, cottony mold; no preservatives, the label said. The refrigerator was empty – as always on a Monday – so no milk and no coffee. Shopping on Sunday was not easy, but not shopping on Sunday led to headaches. He might have stopped at the store in the train station by the Berlin Zoo on his way home from the Delphi Theatre. So what if the prices were a little high. Manfred had said, "If you've gotta pay three times the regular price for a cup of coffee, you're better off drinking tap water." If Manfred was still in Berlin, that might have started another argument, but right now, Manfred was probably sound asleep in his apartment in downtown New York. Maybe he was snoring his usual cat-purr snore. Mamoru wondered if Manhattan at three a.m. was still alive with wailing sirens and the laughter of people walking down the street. Manfred was the kind of guy who, once asleep, wouldn't wake just because of a little extraneous noise. Once, a parade blaring techno music had passed by their apartment, but even that wasn't enough to wake him. As he thought of Manfred, Mamoru's molars begin to throb, and he lost all interest in chewing the hard bread. He opened the cupboard to see what else there was. Behind the brown sugar, which was hard as a rock, and a bag of old trail mix with the label "student fodder," he found some cereal that Manfred must have bought.

Mamoru rattled the box. There was probably a quarter of the box left, but there wasn't any milk. He thought of the childish gestures Manfred would make, sliding his spoon into his bowl at a forty-five–degree angle and opening his mouth absurdly wide when he ate. His cheeks were round and full – it was the only part of him that retained the soft traces of youth. He wore only short-sleeved shirts, even in the dead of winter, which caused the muscles of his forearms to tense up. Once, while asleep, Mamoru had buried his nose in the curly, light brown hair on Manfred's arm, and the tickle inside his nostrils woke him up. Manfred would sometimes flop over in bed in the middle of the night. At those moments, he might knock Mamoru on the cheek, and Mamoru would wake up with a groan. Half-asleep, Manfred would lift up a little and mutter, "What? Someone hit you?" Then, with eyes still closed, he'd lie on top of Mamoru. His weight seemed less like that of a human body than that of a mass of inorganic matter, like a sandbag. "You're crushing me," Mamoru would say, unable to get out from under him. His parts were feeling numb and distant, yet there was a flow of blood that made him hard. Was Manfred moving his hands in his sleep?

Mamoru stood motionless in his kitchen as these thoughts went through his mind. Suddenly looking at the clock on the wall, he kicked himself into gear. His appointment at the dentist was at nine-thirty. His Japanese class at the university was in the afternoon so he hoped the anesthetic would have worn off by then, allowing him to speak normally. He went down to the communal basement to retrieve his bike, which he'd parked there because bicycle thefts were on the rise. As he repositioned his linen bag across his shoulder, he felt something poking him in his side. What could it be? It was a sashimi knife, brand name "Nippon," although it was made in China. He had bought it at a department store last week and had obviously forgotten about it. There wasn't any time to go back into the apartment and leave it there. He imagined falling while riding his bike and stabbing himself – the sort of thing you might see in a manga. But the knife was in a case, so he doubted that would happen. He stepped on the pedal and took off.

The wail of the siren trailed off into the distance, marking what, by coincidence, turned out to be nearly an hour of unbroken silence, but eventually the drunk lying on the side of the road woke up and resumed shouting his monologue, starting up where he had left off yesterday. Another hour, then a compact car drove by, then another, as if the cars were coming out of nowhere. A garbage truck made its way down the narrow downtown streets. Its gigantic metal claw grabbed the trash and tossed the rotten remnants into the huge, gaping mouth on its back. Sounds of breaking glass and crumpling plastic. In his dream, Manfred was lying face down, buck naked, on a wet floor, which seemed to be the deck of a ship. His wrists and ankles were tied up in a fishnet, and he couldn't move. The boatman approached. He leaned down and with his knife poked at the tensed muscles of Manfred's buttocks. He seemed to be checking if Manfred was dead or alive. If he realized Manfred was alive, he'd jam the knife up Manfred's rectum, killing him on the spot. Manfred pressed his abdomen against the damp deck, clenching his teeth, holding his breath; some little fish from the net, however, had found their way underneath him, and they wriggled under his weight trying to free themselves. They were ticklish. How could Manfred stay still with this going on under him? Damn it, hurry up and die. He wished he could crush them, but no such luck. The slightest movement and he'd be done for. The fear and ticklishness were getting unbearable. He was having to squeeze to hold back the contents of his bladder. If he pissed himself, he'd be punished. He'd be strung up in a public square and his ears lopped off with scissors. And then his nipples, and then...

    Fortunately, the alarm clock went off. He always had it set for six. He jumped out of bed and, naked, went into the kitchen where he splashed water over his face. The shower was so old it looked like it was out of the thirties. It hadn't given him any trouble when he first moved to New York, but recently, it had been on the fritz. It wouldn't spit out enough water to satisfy a cat's thirst. In Berlin, it had been his routine to take a cold shower each morning. He'd use

Time Differences

so much water it was like standing under a waterfall. A cold shower helped tighten his drooping skin, and not being about to take one made him irritable. He went back to the bedroom and straightened the sheets and blanket. He found himself growing emotional as he remembered waking up with Michael there. It hadn't been that long ago. On the day they parted, in the airport café, Manfred had cried. He had watched his own large tears fall into his cup of coffee. Michael had watched this too, amazed that such a big, muscular man would cry like that. Did Manfred not know the law governing the ratio between muscles and tears? Michael had been born on the East Coast of the U.S. and had spent his whole life there, but it was now time for him to leave it and Manfred behind. As Michael got up and made his way to the gate, he smiled. He had nothing more than one piece of red carry-on luggage in hand as he boarded the plane. He seemed as happy and carefree as if he were going to visit a cousin in Boston for the weekend.

Manfred had not intended to wait faithfully, but he had already developed the habit, every time he looked at the calendar, of calculating how many months it would be before Michael's homecoming. People invited Manfred to parties, but he had stopped putting in appearances. He couldn't stay in New York forever. He was a student and supported himself by teaching German, but it wouldn't be long before he'd lose his current position as a teaching associate, which put much-needed cash into his pockets. He had heard it was difficult to renew positions like his. If things didn't work out, he'd be forced to go back to Berlin at the same time Michael finally got back to New York. He didn't want to go home anymore. He wanted to find a job in New York and get a green card. He wasn't sure if Michael wanted the same thing for himself in Tokyo, but what if he did? What if he didn't come back from Tokyo? Manfred wondered if there was such a thing as a green card in Japan.

That day he'd go "together" with Michael to the gym – or more properly speaking, they would speak to each other on the phone and confirm that they were both going to the gym at the same time. Despite the distance, they would workout at the same moment – that was what Manfred meant by "together." If it was early in the morning in New York, it'd be nighttime in Tokyo where Michael was. If they went to the gym simultaneously, they could sweat at the same time. Manfred had trouble imagining what a gym would look like in Tokyo so he asked Michael to send him a photo, but Michael hadn't bothered, saying that gyms are the same everywhere. Instead of a photo of the gym, Michael had sent a photo of himself in a light, bedtime kimono, sitting in a Japanese-style room. Manfred had heard of sliding doors made of paper and flooring made of something like woven straw, but was that what he was seeing in the photo? Manfred stuck the picture on the wall, but it only worsened his mood. Michael said he was going to the gym, but he was probably going somewhere like that room instead. Manfred imagined Michael dressed in a kimono with his head propped on his arm, nodding off to sleep in the second home of some low-level manager from a big company. He didn't like the way the kimono was half-open, half-closed. The thing ought to have a zipper or buttons or something. "You're supposed to be going to the gym. What were you up to just now?" Manfred was curt as he barked these words into the receiver. "Huh? Oh, it's you." "What were you doing? Is there someone in your room with you?" "There's no one here. I was drawing my dog manga." "All you do is draw. You're not there to learn how to draw manga." "It's fun. It's easy to get hooked." "Just put the drawing aside and go to the gym. If you don't go work out, it means we won't be doing it at the same time." "Doing it at the same time? You'd think we're having phone sex or something."

Time Differences

Michael begrudgingly closed his sketchbook. He could lie and say he had gone to the gym when he really hadn't. There wasn't much chance he'd be found out. Michael liked the ring of the Japanese word *bareru*, "to be found out." He used to go to the gym a lot in New York, but after being in Tokyo a while, he began to take more pleasure out of going to the public bath in the evening. There, he'd soak in the hot water and gaze abstractedly at the steam rising off the water. Michael had a part-time job teaching at a company so he only had time to go to the gym twice a week, but recently, even twice a week had come to seem like a hassle. He didn't really care if he and Manfred went to the gym "together" or not, but he couldn't bring himself to say that to him. Going to the gym at the same time even when far apart – if they broke that tradition, they'd shatter the illusion they were living in the same moment in time. In reality, the only bond still tying him to Manfred was the telephone. Their bodies never touched. For a moment, Michael was unsure what to do, but in the end, he decided to go the gym after all. He slipped on his white shorts and red running shirt, then headed out from his apartment.

On the sidewalk, a fellow who looked like a businessman, briefcase clutched to his chest, was pushing open the door to a coffee shop when he suddenly stopped midway. It was obvious he was staring at Michael's thighs. Michael stopped, wondering what the man would say, but he didn't say a word. He simply looked at Michael as a thing, ignoring his subjectivity. He might as well have been gazing at a poster. Miffed, Michael spoke to him in a loud and absurdly formal tone, "What part of my lower extremities do you think is the most artistic?" The man turned away, clearly vexed.

There were the same three high school girls hanging out, as always, at the entrance to the gym, and when they caught sight of Michael, they quickly fell silent. Michael went to the gym every Monday and Wednesday evening, so it wasn't impossible that they were lying in wait for him. "Lying in wait," perhaps, but it wasn't as if they would attack or anything. He decided to say something. "If you think I'm a famous singer or something, you've got the wrong guy. I've got one of those faces, but I'm no celebrity." One of the girls, whose face was caked with makeup, burst into a big smile, showing all of her overlapping teeth. "Doesn't matter to me if I do have the wrong guy!" she said. At least this girl had a sense of humour, unlike the businessman.

Five minutes after finishing his workout, Michael had already forgotten which machines he had used. The instant he got on the machines, his body would become part of the mechanism and his brain stopped working. He had set the timer on his wristwatch to go off in forty-five minutes, and when it beeped, he jumped off the machine and made for the locker room. Next door to the gym was a public bath. As he entered through the *noren* curtain in the vestibule, he was greeted by the smiling owner, who had already come to recognize him. In the changing room, Michael peeled off his clothes, damp with sweat. In the bathing area, the only other person was a young man, who was bending over, washing his legs. There were none of the usual chatty old men or cheerfully shouting young boys. Michael sat on the stool next to the young man and splashed a pail of water over himself. He had brought some soap that smelled of cypress, and rubbed it into his long, narrow washcloth before starting to scrub his midsection. He glanced furtively at the young man beside him and realized he didn't look entirely unlike Mamoru.

He had met Mamoru two weeks ago. It was late at night, and he decided on a whim to stop into a bar he had never been to before. There was a single customer in the place, a young man drinking a whisky-and-water quietly at the counter. Michael broke the ice with a lie: "Say, haven't I seen you somewhere before?", then asked his name. The young man explained that he lived in Berlin, but he had come back to Tokyo for his younger sister's wedding. Michael turned the conversation to dogs, but Mamoru grew fidgety and said it was time for him to get going. Michael followed him out the door. Thinking to grab a taxi, Mamoru headed the main road, but the traffic there had ground to a halt. Mamoru didn't look over his shoulder, but he seemed to sense Michael behind him. He walked down a narrow street alongside a convenience store, coming to a dark parking lot surrounded by apartment buildings. Two cats were fighting there, raising a howl that split the night.

Michael remembered the crisp tan lines on Mamoru's buttocks. He wished he had asked Mamoru when he had gone swimming. And with whom? And was the Baltic Sea far from Berlin or not? Later, as Mamoru was leaving, Michael asked him for his email address. Michael had sent three messages, but hadn't gotten any response. Maybe there was someone who kept Mamoru from writing back, or maybe he had gotten caught up in his work at the university and didn't have the time to write back. For the first time in his life he thought he might like to visit Berlin. It wasn't as if Michael had no connection with Berlin whatsoever. When he was young, he learned that his grandparents had owned a house in the Schönefeld neighbourhood of Berlin, but that it had been confiscated when they fled to the States. After the war ended, Germany was divided into east and west, and the east took its time restoring property seized by the Nazis to the rightful owners. After the wall came down and east and west were reunited, Michael's parents often mentioned the possibility of reclaiming the house. Michael asked if they were planning to go to Berlin to see it, but his parents simply shook their heads, no. His mother did say that she remembered going to the Berlin Zoo when she was three. She still could remember the exceptionally smart elephant there. Michael teased her, saying elephants were smart regardless of whether they were in Berlin or Washington, but she insisted that wasn't true; the elephant in Berlin had been very, very bright. The other day, when his mother called him, Michael said, "I've been thinking maybe I'd like to take a trip to Berlin. I'd like to check out those elephants." His mother didn't ask the reason for his sudden interest, but she was clearly pleased. "Really? Well then, we'll buy you the airline ticket for your birthday." Michael found himself dreaming how much fun it would be to go to the zoo with Mamoru, then as closing time approached, sneaking off into the bushes so they could spend the whole night in the park. He pictured the wet hefty legs of the hippopotamus, the bright red penises of the baboons, the sharp antlers of the bucks, the sandpapery tongue of the lioness methodically cleaning the bums of her cubs, the sparkling eyes of the crocodiles that seemed so full of tears... These animal visions filled Michael's mind as he sat in the steaming hot water of the bath. He felt a rush of blood to his head, and he hurriedly got out of the tub. By the time he looked at the clock in the changing room, it was nearly ten.

    At that moment, Mamoru was having a café latte with three students from his advanced Japanese class. The dentist had drilled a molar and had told him to stay away from any milk products that day, but by the time he thought of the dentist's advice, it was too late and the latte was almost gone. Oh well. Still this brought on the memory of how indignant Manfred had been one day: "Some company has gone so far as to control our linguistic habits. The word *milk coffee* has disappeared from all the menus, and you hardly ever see *café au lait* anymore. Everywhere you go, all you ever see is *café latte*." Manfred was so ticked off he pulled out a pen and started scratching out *café latte* on the menu and writing *café au lait* instead. "You're going to America, right?" Mamoru had said to him. "Maybe you ought to go to France instead." There was sarcasm in Mamoru's tone, and Manfred stiffened at this affront. Mamoru thought of this exchange whenever he had a latte.

It was only two in the afternoon, but the café, which was close to the university, was buzzing with students tipping back their beer mugs and arguing loudly about the new system of tuition. Mamoru turned to the three students with him and said to them in Japanese: "The students are on strike today." They responded with worried expressions and a barely audible *hai*. These students of his were not interested in anything in the world other than *kanji* and Japanese grammar. The new system of tuition didn't seem to trouble them at all. When they heard there was going to be a strike to protest the rise in tuition, all they were concerned about was whether the remaining Japanese classes of the summer term would be cancelled. Mamoru had wanted to honour the strike in some way, but he also didn't want to disappoint his conscientious students. In the end, he decided on a middle course: he'd meet his students in the café, and he'd talk in Japanese with them about the strike. That way he wouldn't be breaking the strike, and the students could still practise their Japanese. In the end, however, the students didn't want to talk about the strike at all. They wanted to talk about university life in Japan. "How much are the monthly fees at Waseda University?" they asked. "Can poor people go to university in Japan?" Mamoru answered their questions politely, but his mind kept wandering. Before meeting his students, he had stopped by the post office and bought some stamps with Schiller on them. They were in the display case, and Schiller's gaze seemed to fix on him like a guy wanting a date. Once, at the Marbach Literary Archive, he met someone who explained why the portraits of Schiller were always so handsome.

It seems Schiller had given detailed instructions to the artist on how he should be painted, then requested touch-ups to the parts of his face that he did not like. Mamoru supposed that this wasn't unlike pop singers who undergo plastic surgery to get the look they want. But Schiller's plastic surgery was on the canvas. No scalpel ever cut his face in real life.

On Sundays, Mamoru would write a letter to Manfred. This week, he had sent it using one of the Schiller stamps. And the letter was something different. First, he put green paint on his lips then pressed them onto a sheet of paper. That wasn't enough to satisfy him, so he painted his genitals green and pressed them onto a sheet of letter paper on his desk. He let everything dry before putting the sheets of paper in an envelope and sealing it with glue and Scotch tape.

That was the second letter Mamoru had sent that day. The other was to a woman named Sylvia who had been his student the year before. She had started learning Japanese because she wanted to study the *Kokinshū*, an early-tenth-century collection of verse. Eventually, she got a scholarship to study in Japan and had left three months ago. Since then, she had written to Mamoru almost every day. No doubt the postman thought she was Mamoru's lover, considering all the artsy, brushed calligraphy on the envelopes. The letters did not contain any overt expression of love, but they seemed to imply a great deal with all their allusions to poems and metaphors. Any hidden meaning was lost on Mamoru, however, since he was not well versed in the Japanese classics. He worried that if he didn't pay attention, he might accidentally make her some promise in response. Each time a letter arrived, a heavy feeling came over him, but he wasn't sure how to put an end to the correspondence. He had thought about telling Sylvia he had a lover and that his lover was growing jealous, so he didn't want her to write anymore. Still, she had never overtly expressed an interest in a physical relationship with

Mamoru. If he were to come right out and be presumptuous enough to say something, it might make the situation even more awkward. It was like insisting you couldn't lend someone money when they'd never actually said they wanted a loan. Perhaps it'd be better if he simply described his daily life and just casually mentioned Manfred. Perhaps then she'd realize that Mamoru and she belonged to different worlds. It wasn't, however, an easy thing to casually work in details of his life with Manfred since Manfred wasn't there from day to day. As he sat to write to Sylvia, staring at his fingers and racking his brains, the sight of his hands brought Manfred's rugged knuckles to mind and Mamoru felt a sudden longing. He thought of how, when Manfred stuck his fingers into the entrance of his bowels and wiggled them, Mamoru would think small snakes were slithering inside him, each with a cruel smile on its face. He'd move his hips to make it easier to withstand their assault, but the snakes would move as he moved and exact an even more intense toll. Mamoru found himself wondering if at, that moment, Manfred's thickly jointed fingers were resting quietly on top a textbook as he taught his morning class.

Manfred rinsed the sweat off his body in the gym shower. By half past seven, he had bought a coffee near the subway entrance and was sipping it as he rushed into his building at the university. By eight, he was standing in front of his German class. Ten students had enrolled, but only four were present. "You pay such high tuition. Don't you think it's a waste to come late?" There was sarcasm in his voice, but the students didn't seem to get it. "In Germany, the universities are still practically free, so it's no surprise if students are late, but here...?" No one even cracked a smile. One student, a serious expression on his face, asked: "If they don't collect tuition, how on earth do they run the universities?" "They run it with taxes," Manfred snapped. "Taxes aren't supposed to

be used for war. They're supposed to be used for education."
The students sat uncomfortably, saying nothing. "All right,
what did you think of this?" Manfred waved the day's reading
in the air. "I want you to express your opinions freely," he
said, then fell silent. He wasn't going to open his mouth until
one of the students spoke. I'm not a salesman, he thought.
The students looked at him with the proper expression of
upper-class folks pretending not to notice that a stranger was
unaware of breaking the rules of decorum. They coughed and
blinked their eyes. The reading for the day was a collection of
interviews with a Jewish writer now living in Germany. After
a few moments, a student with a Slavic accent chimed up:
"When I read the first interview, I didn't expect there would
be those sorts of questions. Here's why..." Thanks to this one
student, it seemed like the class would get on track.

    As he listened to the students talk, hunger began to gnaw
at his stomach. He had office hours as soon as class ended.
Students could drop in to talk about whatever they wanted.
No appointments necessary. He'd have office hours until the
department meeting later on. The meeting might turn into
a long one. He was so hungry he felt like his stomach might
cramp. Perhaps he could run over to the bagel shop and have
them throw together a sandwich with salmon and alfalfa
sprouts. But would he have that much time? There was always
a line at this time of day. He'd be in real trouble if someone
spied him at the bagel shop when a student was looking for
him at his office. The students were like customers, and
customers were to be feared. Then he remembered seeing
advertisements for a new, take-out pizza joint. Maybe his only
choice was to have a pizza delivered to his office and to eat it
while he was talking to the students.

    Right then, Michael was at an outdoor noodle stand
eating a bowl of ramen. He slurped loudly as he sucked up
the noodles, which were topped with a mound of thinly sliced,

half-transparent scallions. He'd been on his way home from the public bath and couldn't resist stopping here. It was just after ten o'clock, still too early for the businessmen who'd stop by for a bowlful on their way home from the bars. Michael had a superstition that when he broke apart a pair of chopsticks, if the chopstick on the left came out bigger, the next day would be a good one. When he broke them apart today, however, the chopstick on the right ended up much bigger. "Ugh, a right-wing day," he sighed. He wondered if they had ramen with scallions in Berlin. It would be a little after two o'clock in the afternoon there. Was Mamoru still teaching his Japanese class? Perhaps he had finished his class and gone to eat somewhere. Michael wondered what he ate for lunch. Eisbein and sauerkraut? Surely not. Should he try giving him a call to ask? But Mamoru didn't have a cellphone. Come to think of it, Manfred didn't used to have one either. He said he preferred the tinkling metal of the pay phones in New York. He walked around with four quarters in his pocket, and he'd stick them clumsily into the pay phones with his thick fingers whenever he needed to make a call. But Manfred had bought a cellphone recently. Michael didn't tell Manfred he'd also bought a cellphone because it'd be a hassle if Manfred started calling him all the time. The cook at the noodle stand looked at Michael through the steam and asked, "You want more scallions?" Michael cocked his head slightly and replied, "If I ate any more scallions, I might turn into a priest." Perplexed, the cook let out a "huh?" "You know, 'cause the flower of a scallion is called a 'scallion priest,'" Michael explained. "Because both flower and the head of a priest are round." The cook laughed. "Michael-*san*, I sometimes don't know if your puns are funny or not!" This little give-and-take was just then interrupted by a woman in a brown suit who called out, "Michael-*san*? Is that you?" Michael raised his face from the steamy bowl of ramen. There was something about her that reminded him of Astro Boy. "Do you remember me? My name is Kanagawa. I interviewed you about two years ago when I was writing an article for an English education magazine." Michael scooted to the left to make space for her. "I remember. It's been ages. Want some ramen with scallions? It's really good. By the way, do you know what the *kanji* for 'scallion' looks like?" The *kanji* was difficult enough that most people didn't know it. "You know, you talked a lot about *kanji* when I interviewed you. Since then, I quit the magazine and started my own manga magazine, if you can call what we do 'manga.' It's kind of offbeat." "What kind of manga are you making?"

At that moment, Mamoru was also talking about *kanji* and manga. His student Jan was denouncing a German scholar who had proposed getting rid of *kanji* completely. "A Eurocentric fool," Jan called him. Jan liked *kanji* so much that when he was ten years old, he had put fake tattoos of the kanji for "beauty" and "love" on his arms, then proudly explained the meaning of the *kanji* to his classmates. Hearing that, Mamoru found himself at a bit of a loss. "But if we rely too much on *kanji*," he ventured, "then the Japanese language might grow weak." Jan expressed surprise. "'Rely on'? What do you mean?" "When people write difficult *kanji*, they feel like they've written something magnificent. However, when people say they can only express something by using *kanji*, maybe they don't really understand the thing they're talking about." Silke, a student who wasn't very good at *kanji*, leaned forward and asked for an example. "Okay, there's the word *rachi*, which means to take someone away, right? People use it when they're talking about North Koreans abducting Japanese citizens and taking them to North Korea. The word is difficult and isn't easy for people to digest. It isn't transparent and has ominous connotations. Because we use difficult words like that, people have a hard time understanding what's really going on." "But I think it's because you've got *kanji* that you developed the culture of manga," interjected Tobias, the third student. Tobias had originally started studying Japanese because he wanted to read more manga but now, for whatever reason, he found himself interested in *Konjaku monogatari*, the ancient Japanese collection of stories.

The mention of manga reminded Mamoru of Michael, the American who liked to draw manga about dogs. They had met each other in a bar a little while back when he was in Tokyo for his sister's wedding. Michael had leaned over and asked if he would like to model for a manga he was drawing. He then mischievously whispered into Mamoru's ear that he wanted him to behave like a dog, too. When Mamoru didn't seem to understand, Michael, enjoying himself all the more, explained that he wanted Mamoru to lift a leg and do his business on a telephone pole. Not just act it out, do it for real. Mamoru felt himself blush as he remembered the way Michael's eyes brightened, flashing like the scales on the belly of a fish, and the way creases formed around the corner of his eyes as he laughed. To clear his mind, Mamoru abruptly said to the students, "I'm hungry. Shall we go get something to eat?" His Japanese sounded like it was right out of a textbook. He had no sooner spoken than Jan asked, "Would it be inappropriate to use the expression 'I'm starved'?" Mamoru replied, only half-sounding like a language teacher, "That sounds more macho," as he paid for the students' coffee.

Mamoru tended to eat at the same places: mostly it was the Afghani restaurant across from the Literature Faculty or the Pakistani restaurant beside that. Today it would be the Pakistani restaurant, where the waiters were in their twenties, had black wavy hair, long eye-lashes, and slender waists, and wore black. Mamoru led the students inside and headed straight for the big table in the back. Jan, who was a bit behind, shouted to him, "*Sensei*!" The waiter looked up at Mamoru. Mamoru felt uncomfortable when people called him that, and here he experienced a moment of irritation, realizing the waiter would think *Sensei* was his name. "*Sensei!*" Jan shouted again before adding, "The pocket on the side of your backpack is open." Mamoru took his backpack off and zipped up the pocket. After ordering some tea, the students began talking about their research projects.

Jan said if he got the chance to go to Japan, he wanted to live in a town with a tradition of producing ceramics. Mamoru didn't know the first thing about pottery so all he could do was quietly nod his head. His parents had liked ceramics, but if given the choice, he'd have chosen plastic dishes with the logo of Leo the Lion instead. There was nothing simple or elegant about them – not the slightest whiff of the restrained elegance or rustic simplicity so highly prized in Japan.

Silke wanted to write her thesis on the history of the death penalty. "In Europe, it's possible for people to get sentenced to life in prison without the possibility of parole. In Japan, people can't be sentenced to life without parole. A life sentence would be a light sentence. A heavy sentence would be the death penalty. Japan can't get rid of the death penalty because it doesn't have anything in between. Japan really ought to create life sentences without parole. But if it does, then there won't be any advocates who do their best to save prisoners. The mafia in jail will stop respecting the people who sentence criminals to parole. And then..." Silke's impassioned soliloquy went on and on, spittle flying from her mouth. Mamoru and the other students listened meekly.

The food arrived at their table. They had barely arrived at the restaurant in time for the lunchtime special, which was salad, rice, and grilled lamb on a large plate. Tobias said if he went to Japan, he wanted to find a job as the assistant of a manga artist. Mamoru said, "That might be difficult, but I know a guy who is aspiring to be a manga artist." He promised Tobias he'd ask him about it. Mamoru had finally found an excuse to write Michael an email. Their relationship had been purely sexual, but Mamoru was no good at writing erotic emails, so he had been trying to come up with something to write about.

When Mamoru paid the bill, he met the eyes of the waiter for several seconds. Mamoru wondered if the guy recognized him, since he came there so often. He wished the waiter didn't think his name was *Sensei*, and he racked his brains for a way to start a conversation. Had the guy seen the Pakistani film the theatre behind the restaurant was showing? The waiter shook his head. Mamoru tried to keep the ball rolling, but when he noticed a man in his fifties with a broad face, his thick eyebrows knitted, watching them from the kitchen, he let the conversation drop.

After parting ways with the students, Mamoru made his way to the university library. Several students were making signs and putting up posters in the plaza in front of the building. Because German universities charged no tuition until recently, Mamoru had been able to pay for his living expenses while getting his Master's degree simply by working part-time. Now he was making a living by teaching Japanese, but over the last year, he had been nurturing the secret desire to write a book. That was Manfred's influence. If he succeeded in writing a book, Mamoru would feel like he had gotten something out of their love, even if Manfred never returned to Berlin. As a result, Mamoru was going to the library even more often than when he was a student. On his way up the stairs to the entrance, Mamoru stumbled and let out a cry of surprise, thinking he might fall.

Right then, Manfred was opening a grease-stained pizza box that had just been delivered. He looked intently at the greyish mushrooms and salami floating on top of the cheese. It was so oily that it looked like it had been coated in varnish. The salami reminded him of the cross-section of a human arm; but he nonetheless he bit into a slice with gusto. At that moment, there was a knock at the door. It was Bogdan, who always spoke up in class and whose German vocabulary was also far greater than the other students'. Bogdan was from Bulgaria. Perhaps many people there spoke German, but even so, Manfred could not help giving him a special smile each class. "Mind if I come in?" Bogdan asked politely. "Not at all, come in, come in." Manfred grimaced at his overly affable tone, which reminded him of a salesman. Bogdan looked at what Manfred was eating. "I see you're having pizza. Have you grown to like food in our country?" There didn't seem to be any sarcasm in his voice. In fact, he seemed to be in quite a pleasant mood. Manfred was surprised by the words "our country." Pizza wasn't Bulgarian food, and Bogdan hadn't even been in the States for a decade. Could he really use the words "our country" to talk about American fast food? He mulled the question over but didn't say anything about it. He couldn't really be critical of others; after all it was he who had dug into this pizza. In Berlin, working-class teenagers were the main market for cheap pizzas, so if a friend caught you eating one, you'd feel you needed to make up an excuse. Manfred hurriedly wiped his tomato-sauce-covered fingers on a napkin and took a swig of Coke. "How are you doing?" he asked in a friendly tone. "Well, to tell you the truth," Bogdan began, "I decided not to study in Vienna next year after all. You went to all the trouble to write me a letter of recommendation so I feel really bad." His tone of voice didn't indicate he felt bad at all. "Why'd you change your mind?" "I got an opportunity to intern at the Beijing branch of my uncle's company during our summer vacation. He tells me I might be able to work there after I graduate." "What kind of company is it?" "They export and sell Chinese-made Christmas items in southeastern Europe." "Really? That sounds promising. If you knew about this earlier, you could have studied Chinese instead of German." Manfred could not entirely hide the jealousy that crept into his voice. Bogdan's response, however, showed a great deal of grace. "Chinese is so difficult, I doubt I could've done as well as I did with you. I've been studying German since high school, and it's really fun for me. Thank you for such a good class. Anyway, I don't want to disturb you while you are eating..." He stood up politely and left.

The pizza had grown cold and unpalatable. As Manfred picked up another piece and bit into it, he glared at the phone on his desk. Manfred often cursed that telephone. It was the kind of phone you might expect to see at a poor university out in the sticks somewhere. To make matters worse, it could only be used for calls in the city. He'd have understood if it was only for calls in the country, but in the city? It made him feel like livestock fenced in a pasture. With no other choice, he had recently given in and bought a mobile phone. If he used it to call Michael often, however, his bank account, which was low to begin with, would quickly dip into the negative numbers. When he was in Berlin, he had looked down on poor kids who spent all their money on the internet and phones, but now, he was in a similar situation. He wanted to hear Michael's voice, even if it was only for two minutes. Not bothering to wipe the grease from his fingers, he began pressing the buttons on his mobile: zero one one eight one three... He knew that if Michael picked up, he had to keep it short. But no one was home. It was past midnight in Tokyo, but Michael wasn't back yet. Where could he have gone? And with whom? It hadn't mattered how much he'd tried to persuade him to get a mobile; Michael said he was against them and refused to listen. If he had one now, Manfred could have called and asked where he was. Of course, it's easy to lie over the phone, but Manfred would have preferred a lie to not being able to reach him at all.

Out of the corner of his eye, Michael watched Sakurako Kanagawa eagerly gobbling down her scallion ramen. He poured himself some saké. After a bit, they decided to go somewhere to grab another drink. They walked down one of the busier streets, full of shops and restaurants, and happened onto a fight. Making their way to the front of the crowd of spectators, they saw two men yelling at each another for all they were worth. The onlookers, however, seemed to be enjoying themselves, and whenever the two drunkards said something, they'd laugh. It only made sense they'd laugh: the drunkard who'd picked the fight was a robot. The fellow getting picked on was apparently a street performer pretending to be another robot. The man was speaking in an overly dramatic fashion, as if he were on stage. "You! You wanna fight, eh?" The robot, which had been programmed to speak in a way that sounded like a machine, shot back, "You! You're the bozo who wanted to get into it!" Kanagawa said, "I've seen people act drunk before, but the robot's really got it down. I wonder if it's really responding to the guy or if it's just playing back a bunch of recorded lines." She tilted her head as she said this. Michael replied, with apparent interest, "Oh, it's hard enough to make a robot that walks on two legs, but a robot that can stumble on two legs is amazing. You know, I once tried drawing a manga with a robot as the main character, but it was too difficult. I couldn't figure out a way to make people feel emotionally involved with it." "Really? I remember once when Astro Boy got hurt. I felt so sorry for him that I cried. It was more than just emotional involvement for me. I actually wanted to *be* a robot too." "Really? Why's that?" "Robots don't have sadness or pain, they aren't egotistical, they aren't narcissistic, they're always fair towards others…" The conversation went on. "Robots are pretty great, don't you think?" she said. She knew a pub nearby so they stopped in and ordered some saké. Michael smiled, "I seem to recall you're a pretty good drinker." She replied, "I always say, 'Work and liquor, I can handle as much as they dish out,' but every time, I just zonk right out." After a brief pause, she added, "Michael-*san*, did you know the expression 'zonk out' comes from Indonesian?" Michael shook his head in surprise, but then she started giggling. "Just kidding! Made you believe it!" With that, she lifted her glass energetically. They hadn't really much to drink yet, but already she seemed plenty inebriated. Through the opening in the short sleeve of her blouse Michael could see the slack, white skin just below her underarm. The sight of this made him think of Mamoru's armpits – the jet black, thick, and straight hair. He wished he could caress those armpits forever. It was already quite late, but he thought he'd stick it out with this woman for another hour, then call Mamoru. It was past five in the evening in Berlin, so Mamoru would be going home soon. He could propose they have a drink "together". In truth, they'd just be doing the same thing at the same time. But they probably didn't have the same kind of saké in Berlin that they do here, and they certainly didn't have the same kind of wine here that they have in Berlin. For that reason, the last time they had a drink together, Michael had ordered vodka, even though he didn't especially like it. There aren't too many brands of vodka so you tend to find the same ones all over the world.

    He stole a look at his watch. One-thirty. "You'll have to excuse me," Michael said to Kanagawa, and stood up from his chair. The alcohol had gone to her head. She asked in a loud voice, "Huh, what? You need to take a leak?" The man drinking in the next seat looked at her and frowned in disapproval. "No, I just want to go shake hands with a friend," Michael answered, then disappeared into the back of the bar. When he was alone in one of the bathroom stalls, he pulled out his mobile. Mamoru had asked him for his number so he could call Michael at any time, but he had never had. It rang seven times before Mamoru picked up. Michael played the fool, "Hello, this is the aspiring manga artist in Tokyo," but immediately he sensed a stiffness on the other end of the line. He was in high school when he had learned to differentiate between silences he'd hear in telephone conversations, and even now, he still thought of it as a peculiar ability. Mamoru asked hesitantly, "Where are you now?" "I'm in a toilet stall in a bar. I'm out drinking with a journalist named Kanagawa. A woman. But I called 'cause I want to have a drink with you. You still have the Moskovskaya you bought the other day?" "Yeah." "At exactly 1:45 a.m. Tokyo time, I'm going to lift my glass to you. Let's both down some vodka at exactly the same moment." "Down some vodka?" "Doesn't have to be a big shot. I'm not talking about an entire bottle."

    Michael hung up, went back to his seat, and ordered a shot of Moskovskaya. "This'll be the last one," he declared to Sakurako Kanagawa. "Afterward, I've gotta go home." Kanagawa suddenly seemed flustered. "But go with me back to my apartment at least. It's not too far." Her eyes were bloodshot. Michael nodded and glanced at his watch. It was time. He raised his glass into the air and with a "*Kanpai!*" he drank the contents down in a single gulp. The woman with him clinked her glass with his energetically and shouted "*Kanpai!*" too.

    Mamoru was planning to go to a lecture entitled "The Iraq War and Changes in Language in the Media," so he didn't really feel like having a shot of hard liquor. Michael would never find out if he didn't. That reminded him. Hadn't Michael written in one of his emails that, for some reason, he liked the word *bareru*, "to be found out"? If Michael wanted to fly all the way to Germany to check if he had drunk a shot of vodka, he'd have a long flight ahead of him. He wouldn't get as far as Narita Airport before the day would be over in Berlin. Mamoru didn't feel like he'd really be betraying Michael.

Time Differences

People far away are powerless anyway. Mamoru poured some vodka into a crystal glass, as if he was participating in some kind of mystical ceremony, then glanced at the clock. It was a satellite clock that automatically adjusted itself to precisely the right time, down to the very second. He watched the numbers until the clock indicated exactly five-forty-five, then with a loud, clear voice, he pronounced the word "*Kanpai*!" Instead of pouring the liquid down his throat, however, he poured it on the palms of his hands almost in an act of purification. Then, he washed his hands, hurriedly threw his linen bag over his shoulder, and rushed out of the apartment.

At that moment, Manfred was rushing to his department meeting. With the rise of interest in the Middle East, the decision had been made to hire a teacher of Arabic. Members of the department had been discussing the position for the last month. Should they bring in someone from another country, or should they cherry-pick an instructor from another institution in the States? Should they hire a recent Ph.D. graduate, or should they hire a veteran professor? Manfred had told them candidly he didn't care whom they hired, but no one would forgive him if he missed the meeting. They had whittled down the pool of applicants from over a hundred to fifteen, and each candidate had been asked to send in a video that made the case for why they should be hired, explaining their field of research, their pedagogical methods, and their contribution to the university. Among the videos received, some had distorted images and others where voices weren't entirely audible, while yet others were so overproduced that the candidate might as well have been a pop star. All the faculty could determine from the videos was how different the candidates' video production abilities were; it was impossible to tell how they would differ as teachers. Someone made the point that it was unfair to judge candidates this way. There weren't the funds to invite all fifteen candidates to campus for an interview, however. It was decided that the videos and other documents would be used, as much as seemed feasible, to narrow the pool to five people, and those would be the ones brought in for a campus visit. That was where the meeting ended.

 Relieved that there had been some conclusion at least, Manfred stood up from his chair. Julia, the creative writing instructor who taught fiction, had been seated next to him again. She always seemed to sit next to him in meetings, eager to chat once the meeting was over. Recently she'd told him she had adopted a child. She invited him to come back to her office to look at pictures. Manfred had no eye for babies, but he went back to her office anyway. She had taped three enlarged photos of her baby to the wall, as if they were posters of an actor. It was just a little baby, but already it had tufts of black hair. "I adopted her in Beijing. Beijing was an amazing place." Manfred hesitated for a moment at Julia's declaration then asked, "Why Beijing?" "The Chinese government is the only one these days that allows a single parent to adopt a baby. If you try to adopt a baby from South America, you have to be married, living with your husband, and you have to be young to boot. If you want to adopt from Russia, it's okay to be unmarried, but you've got to have a man in the house. It doesn't matter if it's a brother, father, or whatever. The thing is, I don't have a man living with me." "Why don't you adopt a baby from here in the U.S.?" "There aren't too many babies up for adoption in the U.S. When they are available, often there are problems like fetal alcohol syndrome, drugs, and things like that. That's what happened to my sister when she adopted a child. I'm not sure I could handle something like that on my own. Chinese babies tend to have good personalities and totally cute faces. Plus, they're smart too." Manfred grimaced as he remembered Mamoru's face. Mamoru's face had grown smaller and smaller in

Manfred's memory, and before Manfred knew it, Mamoru had become like a baby. He imagined Julia changing his nappies. Julia nudged Manfred for his approval, "Cute, eh?" No doubt about it, Mamoru was cute. But as a sexual being, Mamoru lacked something in Manfred's eyes. For instance, Mamoru lacked the stick-to-it-ness and courage to torment him over a long period of time in ways that Manfred really wanted. When Mamoru was the one being tormented, he just lay there and suffered, and that was no fun at all. Manfred wanted Mamoru to become more involved, but he just retreated into his own little cocoon. Compared to Mamoru, Michael was smaller and thinner, but he was tenacious and wasn't at all afraid to bring out whatever cruelty he had inside himself. They could sweat together until dawn rolled around, exploring one another's bodies. Even if Michael were to find some blood on his fingers, he wouldn't stop. He'd just as soon lick it off to satiate his appetite.

Manfred suddenly came to, realizing Julia was looking at him quizzically. "But you've got your job here," he said, trying to return to the conversation. "Are you going to be able to raise a baby on your own?" "My girlfriend is a computer graphic designer and she works at home." "Oh! I see. You're not a single mother, you're double mothers. I envy you—" He stopped mid-sentence, not quite sure if he should talk about himself. Had Julia tried to get so close to him just by chance, or did her gaydar pick up on him, giving her a feeling of kinship? As he was asking himself these questions, the telephone rang. Julia grabbed the receiver from the phone on her desk. Manfred decided to take it as a cue to leave. He bid Julia goodbye with his eyes, and left. Back in his own office, he started pressing the tiny buttons on his mobile: zero one one eight one three... He got irritated at this seemingly never-ending string of numbers. He had heard you could store numbers, but it was too much trouble to read the instructions so he didn't know how to do it. No one answered. It was past two in the morning. Was Michael playing around? Spending the night at someone else's place? Manfred felt dizzy. The skyscrapers outside the window leaned to one side, and he felt an unfamiliar space open below his feet. He was falling into a darkness that rose to envelop him. It was daytime. Why was it so dark? Bright petals of flowers spread over his head like fireworks. What on earth was happening?

Michael had been prone to carsickness ever since he was a child. Even the time his father had promised to take him on a fun trip to Florida with his uncle, the first whiff of gasoline had been enough to make him nauseous. Even so, he had got into in the car, thinking how much he wanted to see the dolphins. He had never been carsick, however, since coming to Japan. As he thought about it, he realized he'd never taken a long car ride since arriving in the country, but now he was in a cab escorting Sakurako Kanagawa to her apartment. She had lied when she said it was nearby. The taxi had been driving on the highway for forty full minutes. Eventually, it got off at an exit, continued for a little, then finally stopped. She put some money in Michael's hand, winked at him, and got out. That wasn't especially strange, but he realized what she had given him wasn't a ten-thousand-yen bill but a measly thousand yen. Had she just been drunk and made a mistake? He was stuck. He didn't have any choice but to use the same taxi to get back home. The thousand yen plus all the money he had on him would be barely enough. He worried that if he dug out all the cash he had in his apartment, it still wouldn't be enough. Wanting to save the cost of the highway tolls, he asked the driver not take the highway back. The driver nodded without a word. The car wormed its way through dark city streets, passing the lonely lights of all-night convenience stores. One kerb replaced another. Suddenly, Michael began to feel the contents of his stomach rise into his mouth. He wanted to say, "Excuse me, please stop the car," but moments after he'd said not to take the highway, the driver had started talking nonstop, hardly even inserting a comma or period long enough for Michael to interrupt. "Sure, this is the kind of work I'm doing now, but I'll show the world when the time's right. I'm trying to get ready for the day when I'm not driving a cab no more. I'm telling you this 'cause I can see you're not a run-of-the-mill kind of guy. Know how I can tell? 'Cause I can see what's behind your head – that light shining there. You were born with it. I've been able to see things like that my whole life, but it took me a long time to realize my appointed mission. Wish I figured out earlier what I was put here on earth to do." "Excuse me, could you stop the car?" "Huh? We're not there yet. And we just started talking." "I feel sick. Please stop. Right away." "As soon as you told me back there not to take the highway, I realized I found someone who'd listen." "Please. Stop. I'm gonna mess your car."

 At the entrance to the auditorium where the lecture was to take place, there were four uniformed guards checking bags and patting down the people who had come to listen. The security guard who stuck his hand in Mamoru's linen bag rustled around for a moment before pulling out the encased sashimi knife. He held it high over his head as if in victory. Mamoru was quickly pulled back to reality, and let out a sigh of annoyance. Why hadn't he left it at home? It'd been in his bag since he bought at the department store last week. "Please come with us, sir." He did as he was told. In the backroom where they led him, there were policemen standing by. One of them, a blond guy in uniform, explained, "Someone telephoned and warned us there'd be an attempt on the speaker's life, so we're being extra careful." His tone suggested they were about done with him, but the other policeman – a guy in plain clothes who had a stack of papers on his desk – glared at Mamoru as if he were a criminal.

Mamoru hung his head and instantly realized he'd forgotten to zip up his jeans. If he did it now, he'd only draw more attention to himself. They probably wouldn't notice if he kept his legs tightly together. "Where's your passport?" "At home." "You know you're supposed to have it with you at all times, right?" "Yeah, but no one really does that, do they?" The plainclothes policeman turned over the sashimi knife in his hands and wrote down some numbers. Mamoru realized he was in real trouble. He'd spent his entire life without ever coming into contact with the law. He found himself amazed how quickly one could turn into a criminal. As the gravity of his situation sunk in, the tension went out of his knees, and for a moment, everything went black. "This is just a procedural investigation, but you know the time we're living in. We have to follow proper procedures." The man said this as if to comfort him, taking Mamoru by the arm and pointing out the window with his chin. Outside, a car was stopped. It was the same colour as an army uniform.

    Manfred grabbed at the sill of his office window and breathed in and out. There's nothing wrong, you're in perfect health, the weather is great, everything outside is like always – the words went through his mind clear as day, but he could feel his consciousness slipping away. There wasn't any reason for him to feel faint, but he was aware he was on the verge of passing out. A moment later, he'd be on the floor. His chest was heavy, full of stone, and his legs were growing thinner and thinner. His breath stuck in his throat. He wanted to call out. He caught a glimpse of the telephone out of the corner of his eye, but if he reached out to it, he'd lose his balance. He thought about yelling, but he could not muster his voice. Had his vocal chords disappeared? He heard a siren in the distance. He thought, there was no way it could be coming for me. Or perhaps, just perhaps, could someone out there have already called it for me?

About the Project

Keshiki is a series of chapbooks showcasing the work of some of the most exciting writers working in Japan today, published by Strangers Press, part of the UEA Publishing Project.

Each story is beautifully translated and presented as an individual chapbook, with a design inspired by the text.

Keshiki is a unique collaboration between University of East Anglia, Norwich University of the Arts, and Writers' Centre Norwich, funded by the Nippon Foundation.

Supported by

1 —
Time Differences
Yoko Tawada
Translated by Jeffrey Angles

2 —
Nao-Cola Yamazaki
Friendship for Grown-Ups
Translated by Polly Barton

3 —
Spring Sleepers
Kyoko Yoshida

4 —
Mariko/Marikita
Natsuki Ikezawa
Translated by Alfred Birnbaum

5 —
The Girl Who Is Getting Married
Aoko Matsuda
Translated by Angus Turvill

6 —
At the Edge of the Wood
Masatsugu Ono
Translated by Juliet Winters Carpenter

7 —
Mikumari
Misumi Kubo
Translated by Polly Barton

8 —
The Transparent Labyrinth
Keiichirō Hirano
Translated by Kerim Yasar